Bounce Around Tigger!

Adapted by Ann Braybrooks
Illustrated by Don Williams

 A GOLDEN BOOK • NEW YORK

Golden Books Publishing Company, Inc., New York, New York 10106

Everyone in the Hundred-Acre Wood knows Tigger, which means that everyone knows his bounce.

Tigger is forever bouncing. He bounces from one friend's house to another—from Pooh's to Piglet's, from Kanga's to Rabbit's, from Eeyore's to Owl's—and back again. And he sometimes bounces his friends, which means that he bumps into them—not out of rudeness, but out of pure excitement.

So one day, when Tigger was droopy instead of bouncy, his friends were quite concerned.

"Why, Tigger," said Pooh, "what happened to your bounce?"

"I lost it," mumbled Tigger sadly. "Look, I'll show you." Tigger tried to bounce. But instead of bouncing, his feet stayed planted on the ground and his arms hung at his sides. Even his tail drooped.

"We'll help you find your bounce," declared Pooh.
"Thank you," said Tigger. "You're all real pals."

With Tigger following behind, Pooh and his friends began searching for Tigger's bounce. Just to be safe, they brought along a butterfly net, a large sack, a glass jar, and a pot of honey (in case Pooh's tummy got rumbly).

Suddenly Piglet shouted, "I see something bouncing! Look!
Over there!" The friends hurried after a grasshopper hopping
across a meadow.

Roo caught the grasshopper in his net, then tipped it into Piglet's jar.

"Pardon me," Pooh asked the grasshopper. "I wonder—did you happen to borrow Tigger's bounce?"

The grasshopper crossed its arms and shook its head no.

"Ahem," said Owl. "Need I remind you that he is a grasshopper, which means that he hops? Hopping is not exactly bouncing, you know."

"Oh, bother! I think you're right," said Pooh as he let the grasshopper go.

A while later, over near Poohsticks Bridge, Rabbit thought he saw something bouncing. "Over there!" he shouted. "Under that tree!"

Everyone ran after an acorn tumbling from a tree.

In his haste, Pooh tripped and fell right on top of the acorn. "Oh, dear!" he cried. "I hope that acorn didn't have your bounce, Tigger."

"I doubt it," said Tigger. "My bounce would have bounced out of the way."

All day, the friends searched the Hundred-Acre Wood for Tigger's missing bounce.

Once, Eeyore accidentally kicked a stone and it bounced across the grass. "Sorry," said Eeyore. "False alarm."

"We'll never find my bounce," declared Tigger, dragging along behind the others.

Just then, Christopher Robin shot out from behind a bush. "He's bouncing!" cried Roo. "He's bouncing!"

Christopher Robin bounced toward them on an odd-looking bouncy thing.

As soon as Christopher Robin jumped off the bouncy thing,
Tigger leapt on it and wrestled it to the ground. After some wild
thrashing, accompanied by grunts and a cloud of dust, Tigger lost
hold of the thing and it tumbled to the ground.

"Tigger!" exclaimed Christopher Robin. "What were you doing?"

"I thought that thing stole my bounce," Tigger replied sheepishly.

"Don't be silly!" said Christopher Robin. "It's just a pogo stick."

"I thought so," said Tigger, frowning, "because even though I won the fight, I still don't have my bounce back."

Tigger sat on the ground and hung his head.

"Now, Tigger," Christopher Robin asked, "did you have a nap today?"

"No," answered Tigger, puzzled by the question.

"Did you remember to have a snack?" asked Christopher Robin.

"I don't think so," said Tigger, trying to think back.

"Well, then, that's it!" said Christopher Robin. "Wait here, and I'll help you get your bounce back."

Soon Christopher Robin returned carrying blankets and some of the foods that Tigger liked best. (Pooh would have shared his honey, but he knew that tiggers didn't like honey.) The others had haycorns and cupcakes. Eeyore had some thistles.

After the friends had their snacks, Christopher Robin
handed everyone a blanket. Then they all settled down
for a nap beneath a large, shady tree.

When the friends woke up, Christopher Robin asked Tigger, "So how do you feel now? Has your bounciness returned?"

Tigger took a deep breath. He tried bouncing on one foot. Then he tried the other.

Suddenly Tigger's little jig turned into a bunch of big bounces.
Tigger bounced up and down on his tail and yelled, "Hoo-hoo!
Look at me! I'm back to being bouncy all over!"

"Bounce, Tigger, bounce!" the friends cried happily.
And Tigger bounced . . . and bounced . . . and bounced . . .
and bounced. . . .